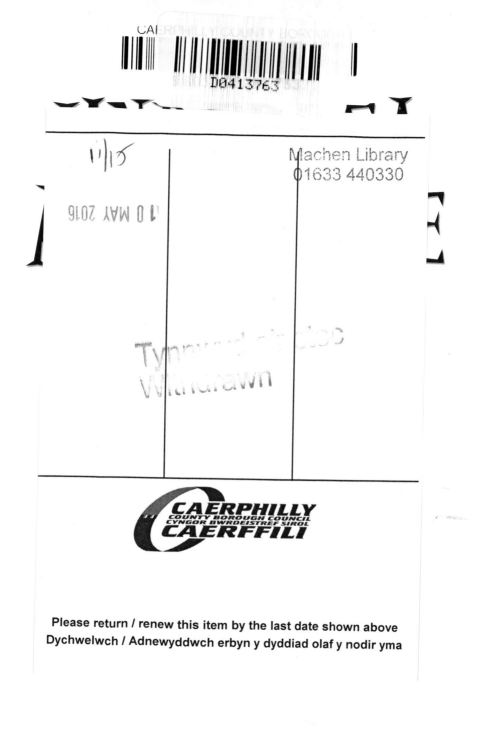

CAERPHILLY
COUNTY BOROUGH COUNCIL
CYNGOR BWRDEISTREF SIROL
CAERFFILI

**Please return / renew this item by the last date shown above**
**Dychwelwch / Adnewyddwch erbyn y dyddiad olaf y nodir yma**

**ReadZone Books Limited**

First published in this edition 2015

© in this edition ReadZone Books Limited 2015
© in text Paul Harrison 2007
© in illustrations Barbara Nascimbeni 2007

Paul Harrison has asserted his right under the Copyright Designs
and Patents Act 1988 to be identified as the author of this work.

Barbara Nascimbeni has asserted her right under the Copyright Designs
and Patents Act 1988 to be identified as the illustrator of this work.

British Library Cataloguing in Publication Data (CIP) is available
for this title.

Printed in Malta by Melita Press.

ISBN 978 1 78322 466 1

**Visit our website: www.readzonebooks.com**

# UNDERSEA ADVENTURE

Paul Harrison
and Barbara Nascimbeni

Swim with me under the sea.

# Whose eye is that?

Whale!

9

Down through the weeds.

Whose arms are those?

# Octopus!

16

Down to the sea bed.

What's in the box?

20

Treasure!

Whose teeth are those?

Shark!

24

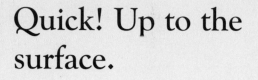

Quick! Up to the
surface.

# Into the boat!

Out of reach, safe on
the beach.

# Did you enjoy this book?

Look out for more *Robins* titles –
first stories in only 50 words

**A Head Full of Stories** by Su Swallow and Tim Archbold
ISBN 978 1 78322 456 2

**Billy on the Ball** by Paul Harrison and Silvia Raga
ISBN 978 1 78322 125 7

**Countdown!** by Kay Woodward and Ofra Amit
ISBN 978 1 78322 462 3

**Cave-Baby and the Mammoth** by Vivian French and Lisa Williams
ISBN 978 1 78322 126 4

**Hattie the Dancing Hippo** by Jillian Powell and Emma Dodson
ISBN 978 1 78322 463 0

**Molly is New** by Nick Turpin and Silvia Raga
ISBN 978 1 78322 455 5

**Mr Bickle and the Ghost** by Stella Gurney and Silvia Raga
ISBN 978 1 78322 472 2

**Noisy Books** by Paul Harrison and Fabiano Fiorin
ISBN 978 1 78322 464 7

**Not-So-Silly Sausage** by Stella Gurney and Liz Million
ISBN 978 1 78322 465 4

**The Sand Dragon** by Su Swallow and Silvia Raga
ISBN 978 1 78322 127 1

**Undersea Adventure** by Paul Harrison and Barbara Nascimbeni
ISBN 978 1 78322 466 1

**Yummy Scrummy** by Paul Harrison and Belinda Worsley
ISBN 978 1 78322 467 8